Sushi the Selfish Cat

Written and illustrated by Kyra Cathcart

Copyright © 2022 Kyra Cathcart. All rights reserved

All rights reserved. No part of this publication may be reproduced, distributed, or transmitted in any form or by any means, including photocopying, recording, or other electronic or mechanical methods, without the prior written permission of the publisher, except in the case of brief quotations embodied in critical reviews and certain other noncommercial uses permitted by copyright law. For permission requests contact

kyracathcartbooks@gmail.com

Instagram (kyracathcartbooks)

This is a work of fiction. Any resemblance to actual events or persons is entirely coincidental.

Edited by Hailey Peterson

ISBN: 979-8-218-00963-2

There were a lot of dangers to being a cat. Cars, dogs, and even hairballs were dangerous, but Sushi was the biggest danger of all.

and she did not share any of her food.

She was the queen of the cats. She planned all the heists and found all the food, but she never got it herself. She made all the other kitties get it for her and she would let them eat it sometimes.

One day, Sushi smelled something coming from a big, pink house. No one had ever gone inside before, but Sushi was absolutely determined.

She had a plan. She made all the other kitties stand up on top of each other and hold her up so she could reach the window.

She jumped inside and what she saw was better than she imagined.

She saw pizza, donuts, coffee, watermelon, and even more donuts!

She ate and ate until her stomach hurt. She had never eaten so much in her entire life! She didn't know what to do with herself. "Maybe I should've let the other kitties eat some of this," she said.

"Grrrrr."

"What was that noise?" said Sushi.

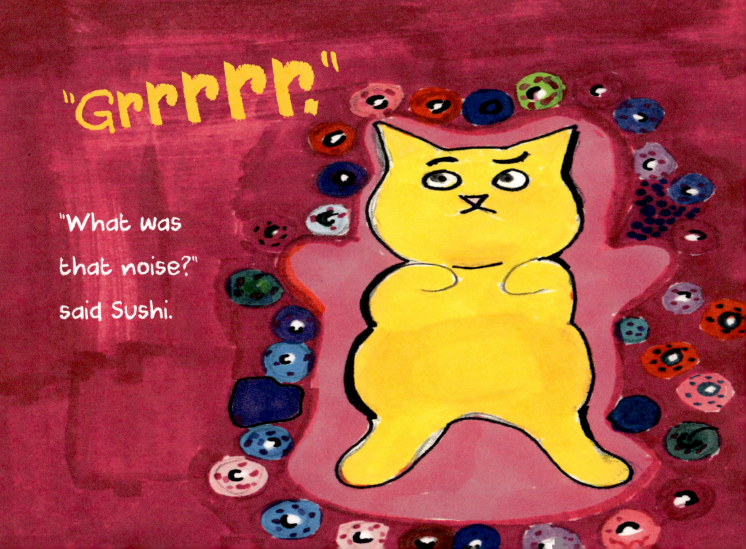

When she got outside, she noticed that none of the other kitties were waiting for her.

She went to go find them and they were eating without her!

She lifted her paw to hit them, but she missed.

"We can't hang out with you anymore," said bushy. "We won't get to eat if we do. Sushi, you're too selfish!" said Brown.

She went to the blue house, the brown house, and green house, and she asked each person for food.

She didn't steal, she didn't bite, nor did she kick. And guess what? They gave it to her!

After she was done collecting food, she had every food a kitty could imagine. She had bacon, eggs, and even donuts! And this time, she was going to share.

Sushi called all the kitties over and placed the food in front of them. She apologized for being so mean and not sharing. "I'll never take your food again," Sushi said.

"We forgive you, Sushi. Would you like to stay and eat with us?" asked Brown.

"Not now," said Sushi. She had somewhere else to go.

Sushi went back to the pink house. As it turned out, the lady in the pink house wanted her to stay.

She loved the house. She ate big meals.

But she didn't forget about the other kitties. She would still eat with them from time to time and she always remembered to share.

Made in the USA
Columbia, SC
31 May 2022